Red Gate

Written By
Tania Tipene

Illustrated By
Amber L. Luecke

A seed tumbles
down a mountain

and lands kaplunk!

She is confused and asks, "Who am I?"

She looks around, "Where am I?"

Seed is afraid.

A voice asks, "Why are you afraid?"

Seed looks around, "Who are you?" she asks.

"I am the Creator, Seed, look around you." the Creator replies.

Seed sees flowers, birds, blue sky, and the Mountain.
"You are at the beginning of your journey home,
Seed. You will learn about happiness on your journey." Says the Creator.
"What is happiness?" she asks.
"Happiness is the feeling of belonging, Seed.
When you feel happy inside, you know you are home.
Go to Mountain, he will guide you."
Seed sets off toward Mountain.

A red gate is across the path.

It is locked!

"Do not fear!" a rumbling voice says.

"Are you Mountain?" Seed asks.

The voice rumbles, "Yes, I am the path home."

Seed looks up. "I have a long way to go." she thinks.

Seed is filled with doubt.

She curls up in her shell and hides.

She is miserable and lost.

Mountain grumbles.

One night, Seed sees a beautiful light above Mountain.
"Who are you?" Seed asks.
"I am Star," a twinkling voice whispers. "I bring hope."
"What is hope?" asks Seed.
Star explains, "Hope is making a wish
and trusting that it will be okay, Seed."
Seed wants to go home where she belongs.
She tells Star that that is her wish.

Star smiles and sprinkles stardust.
Seed is filled with hope and exclaims,
"I can do this Star! I can. Thank you."

The Sun rises over Mountain and fills Seed with energy.

Seed is grateful.

She Salutes the Sun.

Red Gate stands before Seed.

"What have you learned here?" it asks.

"I have learned about Hope." Seed replies.

"Why is Hope important?" asks Red Gate.

Seed replies, "Hope helps me to face Fear.

Without Hope, I would still be hiding in my shell afraid to move forward."

Red Gate has one more question for Seed:

"Why is it important to move forward?"

Seed smiles as she answers,
"So I can find that place where I belong
and feel happy inside."
Red Gate opens.

Seed begins her journey up Mountain filled with Hope.

Mountain rumbles.

Seed leaves Fear and Doubt behind her

as she begins her journey home.

Hello! Seed here. I hope you are enjoying my story. Just like you, I am growing. On my journey through Red Gate, I met characters that are yoga poses, just like me! They helped me grow. Follow along with me, and I will teach you each yoga pose, so you can grow too.

Seed

A seed is just beginning to grow, so I am close to the ground. If you get down on your knees, you can be a seed, just like me.

Press the tops of your feet into the ground gently, and sit back onto your heels.

Now, lift your arms over your head and bring your palms together, so that they sit on top of your head.

When a seed begins to grow, it grows a sprout on top of its head. That is what your hands are! Now, close your eyes, and relax. You will begin to grow straight and tall soon, but for now, relax and breathe.

Do you like to swing on gates? It's great fun. They swing open and closed. At the beginning of my journey home Red Gate was closed. I had to learn my lessons for Red Gate to open, only then was I able to follow my path home.

Gate

On your knees, press the top of your feet into the floor.

Stretch your right leg straight out to the right side with your toes down, and put your hands on your hips. Right now you are a closed gate!

Breathe in through your nose and lift your left arm up to the sky. Then breathe out and lean over, stretching your arm to the right.

You have opened, just like Red Gate did to let me pass. Thank you! Now, try it on the other side.

Can you stand as wide and tall as a mountain?

Mountain

Stand with your feet apart and imagine your feet are a firm base.

Now reach the top of your head up high toward the sky.

Then reach your arms down by your sides.

As you stand tall and steady, feel strong and dependable. I climbed Mountain. As my path home, he needs to be strong. When Mountain rumbles, I feel his strength. Can you rumble just like Mountain?

Next time you see a star in the sky, make a wish and hope that it will come true. You know I did!

Star

Stand in Mountain pose and reach your arms up and out to each side.

Then, balancing on your right leg, reach out with your right arm and lean in that direction.

Finally, lift your left leg up stretching it out towards your left side.

You are a star! Make that wish and maybe you will be sprinkled with stardust too. Try it on the other side and have fun!

When the Sun rose above Mountain, I lifted my arms, and was filled with energy. It made me feel glad inside. Try it, so you can feel glad inside too.

Salute the Sun

Start in Mountain pose.

Breathe in...

With a big breath in through your nose, lift your arms up over your head and stretch up to the Sun.

Breathe out...

Then breathe out and lower your arms down to your sides.

It's simple to do and makes you feel good.

Now that you know all the poses, let's put them all together! Make sure you breathe in and breathe out, and have fun!

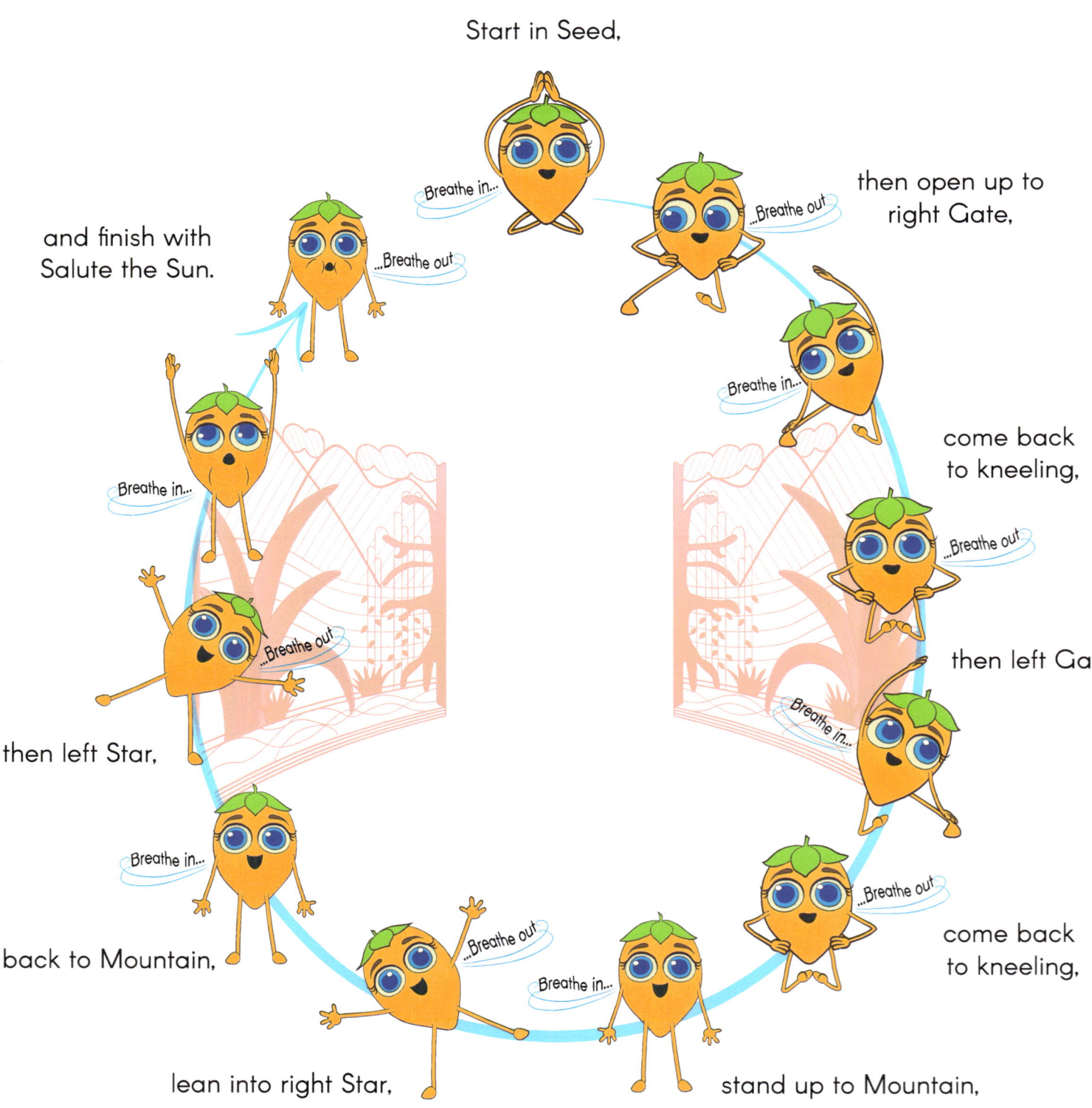

Start in Seed,

Breathe in...

...Breathe out

then open up to right Gate,

Breathe in...

come back to kneeling,

...Breathe out

then left Gate,

Breathe in...

and finish with Salute the Sun.

...Breathe out

Breathe in...

...Breathe out

come back to kneeling,

then left Star,

...Breathe out

Breathe in...

back to Mountain,

...Breathe out

Breathe in...

lean into right Star,

stand up to Mountain,

Follow Seed on the next part of her journey...

Orange Gate